An I Can Read Book™

# THE OCTOPUS

By Denys Cazet

Grandpa Spanielson's
## CHICKEN POX STORIES
story #1

HarperCollins*Publishers*

HarperCollins®, 📖®, and I Can Read Book®
are trademarks of HarperCollins Publishers Inc.

Library of Congress Cataloging-in-Publication Data
Cazet, Denys.
The octopus / Denys Cazet.— 1st ed.
p. cm.—(Grandpa Spanielson's chicken pox stories ; story #1) (An I can read book)
"Level 2."
Summary: Grandpa helps his favorite grandpup to avoid scratching his chicken pox by telling
how he once had to fight off an octopus during a terrible storm.
ISBN 0-06-051088-9 — ISBN 0-06-051089-7 (lib. bdg.)
[1. Dogs—Fiction. 2. Chicken pox—Fiction. 3. Sick—Fiction. 4. Grandparents—Fiction.
5. Octopuses—Fiction. 6. Storytelling—Fiction.] I. Title. II. Series.
PZ7.C2985Oct 2005
[E]—dc22
2003026557

1   2   3   4   5   6   7   8   9   10
❖
First Edition

*For Mike Kauble
and the girls,
Juanita,
Azalea, and Brianna*

Doctor Storkmeyer
closed his black bag.
"Chicken pox!" he said.
"This pup has the chicken pox!"

Grandpa shook his head.

"He has more spots

than a dalmatian."

"It itches, too," said Barney.

"A warm bath will help,"

said Grandma.

"And here's some lotion,"

added the doctor.

"How long before he's better?"

Grandpa asked.

"The fever will go away soon,"

said the doctor, picking up his bag.

"Give him warm, soapy baths
and plenty of rest.
The rash should go away
in a few weeks!"

9

"A few weeks!?" cried Grandpa.
"My favorite grandpup
has to itch for weeks?"

"That's how long it takes,"
said the doctor.
"I can cure him faster
than that," said Grandpa.

Doctor Storkmeyer laughed.

"I've known you for seventy years!

You couldn't cure a ham.

I'll see you tomorrow."

Barney sat up.

"You know how to cure

the 'Chicken Pops,' Grandpa?"

"Easy," said Grandpa.

"And I can do it for free!"

"How?" asked Barney.

"I'll drive them out

with my famous anti-itch

Chicken Pox Stories."

"Go ahead, Grandpa.

I'm burning up!" said Barney.

Grandpa sat on the edge of the bed.

"Once upon a time . . ."

"Don't start now," said Grandma.

"This boy needs a warm bath."

Grandpa went into the bathroom.

He filled the bathtub,

and Barney climbed in.

"Does that take some of the itch

away?" Grandma asked.

Barney nodded. "A little.

Maybe Grandpa should try

one of his anti-itch stories."

Grandma rinsed the top
of Barney's head with a sponge.

"I'll be back," she said.

Grandpa winked at Barney.

Grandma raised her right eyebrow.

"No scary stories!" she added.

Grandma closed the door.

"Okay, Grandpa," Barney whispered.

"Start driving out the itches!"

Grandpa rubbed his hands.

"Okay," he said.

"Let's start with a scary story!"

Once upon a time,

in the olden days,

when Grandma was much younger,

we lived by the sea.

One night

there was a terrible storm.

The sea turned wild.

Waves pounded the shore.

It rained so hard the roof rattled.

The wind howled

and the shutters banged.

There I was,

sitting in the bathtub,

minding my own business,

when it happened.

The bathwater turned dark.

Bubbles oozed.

The bathtub shook.

The pipes rattled.

YOW!

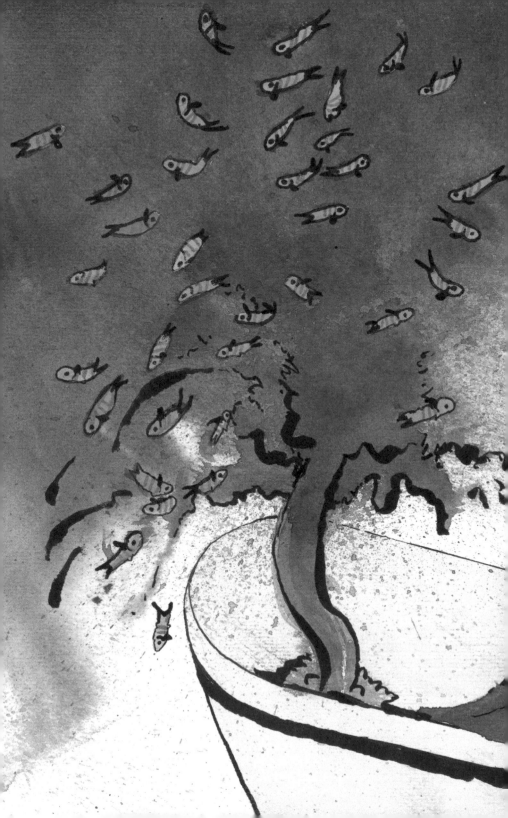

A hurricane burst out of the drain.

The wind whistled

and thunderclouds roared.

Fish rained from the ceiling.

I was almost run through

by a falling swordfish.

The storm got worse.

I tried to get out

but something grabbed my tail.

It had a head like a giant sponge

with eyes in it.

Its beak snapped at me.

HEY!

"Octopus!" I shouted,

and whacked it with the swordfish.

The octopus grabbed

another swordfish.

We had a sword fight.

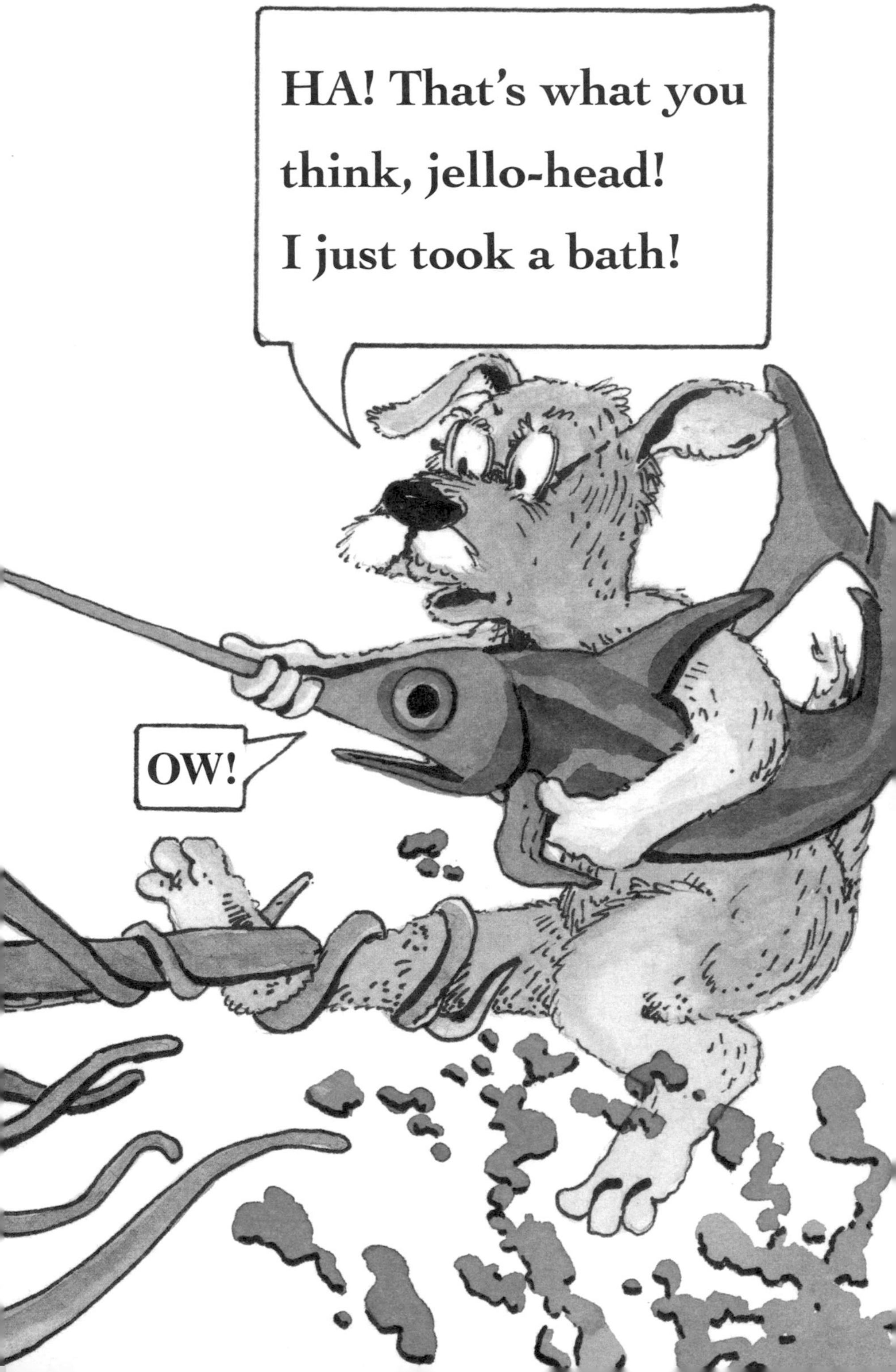
HA! That's what you think, jello-head! I just took a bath!
OW!

The octopus

threw the swordfish at me.

I grabbed the toilet plunger

and *squooshed* him!

*Squoosh, squoosh, squoosh!*

He tried to drag me down the drain.

*Squoosh, squoosh, squoosh!*

Suddenly, the water washed down

the hole and the storm ended.

The octopus was gone.

I looked out the window.

The sea was calm.

That night

we had swordfish for dinner.

"Wow!" said Barney.

"That was a good anti-itch story.

I feel better already!"

"Yes," said Grandpa.

"My famous anti-itch stories are . . ."

Grandpa stopped. He gasped.

"What?" said Barney.

"Don't move," Grandpa said.

"Why?" Barney asked.

Grandpa pointed at the sponge
floating in the bathwater. "Look!"

"What?" said Barney. "The sponge?"

"That's not a sponge!" said Grandpa.

"What is it?" Barney asked.

"OCTOPUS!" Grandpa shouted.

"OCTOPUS!" Barney shouted.

"I'LL SAVE YOU!" Grandpa yelled.

He jumped into the bathtub.

The plug popped out

and the water drained away.

Grandpa held up the sponge.

"Its legs are gone," said Barney.

"The 'octos' must have gone

down the drain," Grandpa said.

"Now it's just a plain 'pus.'"

Grandma opened the door.

"GOOD HEAVENS!" she cried.

"What happened?"

"Octopus," said Grandpa.

"Octopus," said Barney.

Grandma stared at Grandpa.

She raised her right eyebrow.

"Most people," she said, "take their

shoes off when they take a bath!"

Grandpa stepped out of the tub.

His shoes squished

as he walked over to the closet.

He took out a mop.

"Octopus," he muttered.

Grandma wrapped

a towel around Barney.

"Put your pajamas on," she said,

"and I'll come tuck you in.

Are you feeling any better?"

"A little," said Barney.

"Grandpa's story helped.

It was about an octopus."

"Did I ever tell you about how I saved Mrs. Piggerman's life?" Grandpa asked.

"No!" said Barney.

"Well, when I was fire chief . . ."

Grandma raised her right eyebrow.

"Later!" she said.

Grandpa winked at Barney.

Grandpa hummed as he mopped.